SUSAN BLOOM

Girlfriend's Guide To Heartbreak

This book is dedicated to my Spice Girls. They are the strongest, most caring, bad ass girls, I know, and I am forever thankful for them, and the stories they provided me.

It's also dedicated to all of the men or women out there who have been dis-loyal, abusive, or just a straight-up lousy person. Thank you for teaching those you hurt that they deserve better.

Xoxo.

Contents

Preface

Hey, there incredible human being. If you're reading this book, you are either looking for a fun read, or you've had someone break your heart. If it's the second one, you're in for a real treat. Each chapter in this book is based on someone's true story about heartbreak and how they overcame what feels like the impossible.

Before you dive in, let me tell you a secret....

Get closer...

Closer...

Woah Woah, too close, how are you supposed to read the page?

Anyways, the secret is that almost every single person in this world has gone through some heartbreak. The best part? They survived it and came out even stronger. How? You may ask. Welp... let's read on and find out!

Once a Cheater, Always a Cheater

I met the other girl. The other girl that I had a bad feeling about for months. We met at a party. She was there with him, and I was not. That stung more than imaginable. But the plot thickens. I met this wonderful girl that had been cheating with the love of my life and then was told that "I" was crazy! Ha. Guess I am! So my crazy self decided to be the better person and give him a chance to explain even though it was far too late for that. His explanation… We needed to break up because he is moving to New York, and I am staying in Georgia. Uh, so what does that have to do with the slut whom you were cheating on me with? Cool beans. So that happened.. on the fourth of July. HAPPY FUCKING BIRTHDAY AMERICA. The problem is, though, I still love him.

It's unfortunate when you realize that you can't trust a single statement coming from someone who you used to believe with your life. You used to tell this person everything, all of your secrets, knowing that he wouldn't say a word to anyone. You could care less about who he was texting or seeing on the weekends because you knew that whatever he was doing was just fine. You could sleep at night without hearing from him because you knew he was probably just busy with his friends. You would get in the car with him every day knowing that you would be safe and that he would never let anything happen to you.

Then it happens. The breaker to all trust, him cheating. He cheats and then tells you as a side note months later because he couldn't be a man enough to do it right after it happened. He tells you and then makes it seem like it's your fault in some mind-blowing way. You can't even breathe. That person who you trusted held in one of the biggest lies possible. It's only the first time, and he's SO sorry, so you slowly start gaining trust back. You work it out and end up staying with him. Big mistake. Why? Because he does it again. This time he's pretty much dating the other girl. You ask him for the truth, and what does he say? "She's just a friend." You try and do everything you can to believe him, but something in your gut knows he's lying.

Then he gets caught, caught right in the act. You knew it. There goes all possible trust after that one. You love him, though, so you try and work things out. All he does is start lying to you about everything because he knows he can get away with it. You do everything you can to try and be what he wants, so he will never do that to you again. You become miss perfection. What does he do, though? He dumps you because you start obsessing over trying to trust him and be his dream girl. You can't believe it. All the hurt he put you through, and he's the one who ends it. You know you should have done it, but unlike him, you cared about the relationship, your mistake. He moves on, perfectly happy knowing that someone loved him, and he can still have any girl he wants. Meanwhile, you try and move on understanding and remembering what he did to you and that your trust for anything will never be the same. You can never have full faith again because it was already shattered so severely.

That was me. I was that girl who allowed someone to mistreat her for so long. I was the girl that gave up her virginity to make sure he stuck around. I was the girl who cried in the bathroom because her boyfriend cheated ON HER BIRTHDAY. That was me.

He was my first love and well my first everything. We met in 2010 at the beginning of my tenth-grade year and started officially dating that October. I had never had someone hold my hand in the hallways or tell me that I was beautiful over a text message. I had never had a guy tell me he loved me, even though now I know it wasn't real love. I fell so hard for him so quickly and lost who I was ever quicker.

The first year of our relationship was pretty much smooth sailing. Then came my birthday, the day he decided to cheat on me with another girl and then tell me about it. That was the day I started to see him in a different light. I no longer saw him as my perfect boyfriend but saw him as someone who didn't think I was good enough, not to cheat. It made me crazy, made me insecure, and made me work so hard to please him that I lost everything I was or could have been.

My trust was gone entirely, and all I could think about was him cheating on me again. I guess I felt it so much that it came true, because sure enough, he did. He cheated again with a girl at our high school. A girl who became friends with me so I wouldn't suspect that she was sleeping with him behind my back. A girl who sent him naked pictures and made love to him while she was on the phone with me. A monster.

That should have been it, that should have been where I swallowed my pride and walked away for good, but I didn't. I continued to fight for someone who was never worth fighting for. I should have been fighting for myself instead, but that would have been way too easy.

By 2014, my toxic relationship was still going…kind of. We had graduated high school and planned to enjoy the summer together before going off to college. In my mind, I thought that meant enjoying time together as a couple, but, in his mind, it meant enjoying any female that gave him the slightest bit of attention.

On July 3rd, 2014, he and I decided to go to a party with some friends. The party was way bigger than we expected, and we quickly lost each other in the crowd. I remember looking for him everywhere and noticing that my friends were all acting strange, trying to keep me away from going outside. We hadn't been there for more than an hour at that point, but that was all he needed to swoon some random girl — the reason I had been blocked from going outside.

There they were, making love on the trampoline, acting like

nobody else was around. There I was, watching him with another girl, not being able to take my eyes off of the scandal. At that point, I was done. I was exhausted, and I was embarrassed. I finally did something that I should have done three years back, I left. I left the party. I left all my "friends," and I left him…for good.

As hurt as I was for being used, lied to, pushed aside, and forgotten about by someone I gave everything to, I planned to take a step back. I didn't need him to put me first. Not if I put myself first. From then on, I realized that I didn't need a guy to do anything for me, and I certainly didn't need to be anything for a guy.

I know I'm beautiful, enjoyable, and kind, and I can tell myself that. I can make myself dinner and fix things when they break, almost as quickly as I can pump my gas and pleasure my self. Why? Because I am great. I am great, and I loved him more than any girl out there is going to, and it's going to be quite funny when one day he realizes that he will never have that ever again. His loss for leaving it behind.

Where am I now? I'm in my successful career, helping children who need it and deserve it. I'm living with the most amazing guy who has never made me question his faith to me. I found the right guy. The right guy who hasn't lied to me, used me or gave up on me like it was nothing. The guy that I love more than anything and didn't think I ever could. I won because I'm great.

Guess what else? You're great too.

"He is not the sun. You are."

— *Christina Yang*

Choose Me

*O*ne of the hardest things to do is to watch someone you love, love someone else. Another super hard thing to do? Walk away from your best friend because you're in love with him.

I met him during college. We will call him J. Within no time at all, J soon became my best friend in the entire world. He was everything. I instantly had feelings for him which scared the crap out of me and excited me all at the same time. The best part was that he had feelings for me too. Then, he came at me with the cold hard truth, he was thinking about getting back together with his ex-girlfriend — this beautiful blonde with bright blue eyes and big boobs.

I never honestly thought I had a chance, but I begged anyways. I asked him not to get back with her and to give us an opportunity as a couple. I spent hours laying next to him, explaining why I should be the one he chooses in the end. At that time, he was confused and very dramatically felt the need to take some time to think about his next move; leaving me alone with my feelings and terror that his decision wouldn't be in my favor.

"We just have so much history together not to give it a second chance."

That's what the TEXT read when J told me that he had made his choice, and it wasn't me. My heart instantly broke, and I felt like I had lost one of the most important people in my life. I felt like I had run in a race without a single sip of water and was tripped right before the finish line. Beautiful blonde: 1 Me: 0.

I couldn't seem to live my life without him no matter what, though, so we stayed friends. Best friends. Those best friends that know everything about each other and fight like a married couple. We'd have slumber parties and movie nights and complain to each other about our love lives. The beautiful blonde didn't live in the same town that we did, so we spent as much time together as possible, and hoped it didn't cause a problem... until it did.

I will never forget the night that he confessed how much he loved me. How he wished he was with me instead of her. How he held me the rest of that night like he was never letting go, but then he let go again. He chose to stay with her even though he loved me. Twice I had been heartbroken by this boy, but I couldn't lose him in my life. So months went by, and I finally decided it was time for me to try and move on. I decided on an online date.

It was Christmas Eve, and I had made plans to go on a date with a charming, super hot guy. He had those dimples you could get lost in, and blue eyes that looked like the ocean in Aruba. He asked me to go Christmas shopping with him so he could find a gift for his younger sister. Automatically, I thought it was adorable that he wanted to get her the perfect gift and that he wanted me to be the one to help him pick it out.

When we got to the mall, I asked to see a picture of his sister so I could try and get an idea of her style and such, unprepared for what I was about to see. The second my eyes hit the picture he pulled up, I felt like I was going to toss my candy canes. It was her. It was the beautiful blonde with big boobs that the love of my life was dating. The girl that had everything I ever wanted. She was my date's sister. Crap.

I tried to play it cool and act as if I had never seen or heard of her before in my life. Instead, I excused myself to go to the restroom…so I could call J and explain what I had gotten myself into. After realizing I wasn't joking, he told me to abandon ship, to make the date so miserable that he would never call me again. I pondered it for a second and then did what anybody else would have done in a situation like that. I rolled my eyes and decided that he couldn't tell me what to do or who to date. Blondie's brother was cute and sweet, so gosh darn-it I was going to enjoy myself.

So I did. I enjoyed myself so much, our dates started to become a regular thing, and about a month later, they became an official thing. As long as neither he or his sister found out that I was secretly madly in love with J, or even knew him for that matter, it would be fine…until it wasn't.

J and I's college decided to put on a concert with an impressive performer. I was so excited about it that I had invited my boyfriend without even thinking twice about the consequences. Oh, and there were indeed consequences. While I had a date for this concert, so did J. My date's sister. Double crap.

Amazingly, we got through the concert without any sight of J and blondie. Soon enough, we had made it through the whole night without spotting his sister and uh, the guy that I never met before in my entire life. Then, the next day arrived, and my luck had worn out. Naturally, Blondie wanted to see her brother since they were in the same town so what better of an idea than to have a double date. Oh boy.

I never knew what an awkward situation was until lunch that day. Not only did I have to pretend I didn't recognize Blondie's boyfriend, but I also had to sit across from him while he retold stories that I had already heard. Even worse, I had to pretend like seeing him with his beautiful girlfriend didn't completely shatter my heart, which it did, into a billion pieces. What does one typically do when their heart hurts? They cry. Oh yes, I started to tear up and had to excuse myself from the booth that felt like it was getting smaller and smaller.

Luckily for me, the only person who noticed my sudden eyeball tears was J. He figured needing to go to the bathroom at the same time wasn't suspicious, so he excused himself as well, to run after me. The second he found me, I instantly fell into him, losing all control I had left. I couldn't do it. I couldn't pretend anymore that I was happy in my relationship and really couldn't pretend that I didn't know someone I was madly in love with.

So my relationship with Blondie's brother ended. I told him everything, and to my amazement, he took it well and promised not to mention it to his sister. J, on the other hand, was still rocking the coward award and stayed with his girlfriend. Shake my freaking head. The boy was going to be the death of me and the reason I died single and alone.

I needed to get some space from him, which I didn't want to do, but I had to do it for my sanity. I told him I needed a best friend break, cleared out my pajama drawer in his room, and went on my lonely way.

It wasn't until the summer that our communication started back. He called to tell met that Blondie had broken up with him. I tried so hard not to sound excited, I did, but oh man was I pumped. He, however, wasn't as pumped. He was hurt and certainly not ready to jump into another relationship any time soon. I was okay with that but made it my mission to be the next relationship when he was ready.

I remember the day like it was yesterday. September 18th, my best friend in the world sat me down to tell me something that was on his mind. He told me that he was ready to love me. He had loved me all along and was prepared for the long haul. I remember crying tears of joy and just wanting to study every detail about him, because he was going to be mine forever. I was ready to plan a wedding then and there — jokes on me.

October 10th, my best friend in the entire world sat me down again to tell me something that was on his mind. He told me that he couldn't love me the way I deserved. He told me that he tried, but he just couldn't get passed us being friends. The third time was the charm to break my heart I guess because I told him to piss off. Our friendship was so exhausting, and I couldn't do it anymore. That was the final straw, and the last time I was going to let him hurt me. In reality, him telling me he didn't love me was the best thing he could have done.

His hurtful words allowed me to move on, finally. They allowed me to meet the real love of my life who never questioned how he felt about me and never took back his love for me. Although my heart took numerous bullets, it grew from the pain and learned to love again.

I lost my best friend in the end, and I miss him every day, but I have learned that it is healthier to remove toxic people from your life, no matter how much you will miss them. It's been over three years now, and I can honestly say I wish him the very best, and smile at the happy memories we shared through our college years. You win some, and you lose some.

* * *

"I am a museum full of art but you had your eyes shut"

— *Rupi Kaur, Milk and Honey*

"Hey Stephen" – Taylor Swift

*F*reshman year; I was the new girl in a public school and had no idea who I even was yet. I knew I liked music and hated math. I knew I liked boys with flippy hair but didn't know how to make out or even hold someone's hand properly. Boys looked at me, but never like they looked at the cheerleaders or the blondes with big boobs. I settled for the ones who I knew liked me because I figured that was the best I could get. Then came Stephen.

He used to stand at his locker, which was right across from my biology class every morning and talk to his friends. The minute I saw him, I knew I had to somehow get him to acknowledge me. He was perfect. Dark flippy hair, a Doors sweatshirt, skinny grey jeans, and a smile that made me melt. My dream guy. Someone who could never like the life of me. Then the weirdest thing happened. He found me on Facebook (when it was still the cool way to chat). He messaged me, asking if I knew this guy who I had grown up with. Our mutual friend had mentioned to him that I had just started at Dunwoody, and he should introduce himself to me. SO HE DID. I couldn't believe it that my crush had noticed me…

Weeks went by of random texts, and him sometimes saying hi to me before my biology class. My friends and I had given him a nickname, "McYummy." Random texts turned into conversations and then conversations turned into hugs in the hallway. Progress! Then… it happened. He asked me to "hang out."

We chose to go to a friend's house, so it was an interactive environment that both of us could feel comfortable. Little did I know that it wasn't just going to be him and I, but his two best friends as well. Not quite the first hang out I was wanting, but hey it was something. We watched a movie, although I can't remember what movie it was. I was a little distracted. Oh, and did I mention my dad was there too? Yeah, he was hanging out with our friend's dad, aka spying on me. Since we had the adults in the other room, we had to keep everything PG, not that I wasn't planning on doing that anyway, but still. I scooted a little closer to him and HE GRABBED MY HAND. MCYUMMY WAS HOLDING MY HAND. I knew I could die happy. Then, the hang out session was over.

His friends became my friends after that night, and well.. so did he. My FRIEND. I knew I was in the wrong zone when he started talking to me about the new hot German exchange student that he wanted to ask out. So he did. I was out, and the German exchange student was in. I'm not one to give up though, so I figured the closer we got as friends, the more likely

14

he would be to fall in love with me...Wrong. We became BEST friends. The type of friend that you did everything with and called every night but never once said anything about "feelings." My side wasn't a secret, though, he and everyone else in the world knew how I felt about him. I guess I'm not very good at hiding my emotions; or maybe it was the fit I threw when he got yet another girlfriend that wasn't me...

Two girlfriends and a lot of mixed signals later, it was summer. We planned a trip to the lake. Me, him, his friend, and my friend. This was going to be it. It had to be. We spent the day riding the jet ski together and laughing at each other's terrified faces on the tube — a long, fantastic, tiring day. I went up and laid down in my bed, contemplating what to do next to get him to see me as more than a friend. Right as I was about to get up and head back down to the dock, he walked into the room. With a smile and a giggle, he laid down next to me. I turned my head to stare into his big brown eyes, and he grabbed my hand. A shiver went up to my spine. This was it. I swallowed every fear I had and closed my eyes, waiting for his lips to touch mine finally. After months of wishing, the day finally came. We kissed for what felt like hours, and every second of it was like a dream. I was finally getting what I wanted...or so I thought.

I fantasized about that kiss for weeks, wondering what was going to happen next. After three weeks passed, I began to lose hope again. It was just a kiss. A moment of weakness on his part. He didn't want me and I was devastated. At that rate, I wasn't this little freshman who took what she could get; I fought for what I wanted. I confronted him for playing with my heart. That turned into a fight that went too far and an ending to our friendship...for a while.

The summer was almost over, and Stephen and I had hardly spoken. I thought about him always and walked around with a sinking feeling in my stomach, but I was too stubborn to fix it. Two stubborn people do not go well when it comes to arguments. Finally... I cracked. I asked him over to watch a movie with me. I was ready to make peace even if it meant going back to being friends. He came over and we clicked instantly again like nothing ever happened. I was just happy to have my best friend back at that point with slight hope for more, of course.

Our movie day was almost over, and we were back to our usual selves. He looked at me and kissed my cheek, which gave me goosebumps. Then the biggest plot twist of the day took place. He whispered in my ear, "will you be my girlfriend?.." I don't think I have ever said the word "yes" that fast in my entire life. After a long, dramatic, exhausting, ten months, I was finally Stephen's girlfriend.

That lasted a week.

Ten months I spent trying to get this guy to finally notice me, only for our relationship to last a week. We just weren't meant to date. Once things became official, we became strangers. We didn't know how to talk to each other anymore and spent less time together than we had when we were just friends. It was weird, and I missed him. I lost my best friend while he was my boyfriend. Huge red flag.

It's been ten years now, and Stephen and I are still excellent friends. We were by each other's side through every heartbreak, awesomeness and whatever else life threw at us. We joke about that time that we tried to date and failed miserably. I don't regret it one bit, though. I spent so much time pawning over him when we were friends that I was unable to take advantage of the friendship part. He was my favorite person in the entire world before we tried to date and sometimes you don't have to date your favorite person in the whole world. Sometimes you need them in your life no matter what the label.

I regret letting myself feel like I wasn't good enough for Stephen when he chose numerous girls over me. I made his opinion and judgment affect how I felt about myself, and I learned that it doesn't get you anywhere but into a dark hole. The truth of the matter is, he did choose me over numerous girls. He chose me to be his first phone call when something significant happened, or his movie-watching partner when he wanted someone to hang out with. He chose me to be his lifelong friend, and I would take that any day.

* * *

"Learn to be alone and to like it. There's nothing more freeing and empowering than learning to like your own company."
— *Mandy Hale*

Do I Know You?

*I*n high school, I started dating my very best friend. He wasn't the best looking guy, but he made me laugh and was always there for me. When I finally realized that I was in love with him, I swore that he was the one I was going to marry. The only issue with dating your best friend, though, is all the baggage they know you have. That being said, he warned his mom about said baggage, causing her to dislike me before she even got to know me.

I've had it rough. I was abused, taken advantage of, and held it inside for so long that I didn't think I would ever get the courage to tell anyone about what I had gone through. When it came to him, though, telling him about my past came easy. I felt safe, loved, and taken care of. He took what I told him and made it his mission to comfort me to the best of his ability. It was all fine and dandy until he opened his big ole mouth and somehow turned his mother entirely off of me.

When I say she disliked me, I mean she 100% disapproved of me. I spent almost a year fighting that disapproval, but she got desperate and did what any mother would do… she bribed him with money to break up with me. Typical, I know.

Amazingly that's not even the best part. See, he had always been a coward, so when it came down to having to break up with me, he decided to make it as easy on him as possible. You can't break up with someone if you don't even know who they are…

Oh yes, he "had" Multiple Personality Disorder. He supposedly had two different alias', one who had been dating me for almost a year, and the other who "had no idea who I was."

Me being the loving and caring person I am believed him for just the slightest second. I decided that if he were telling the truth, I would have to make his other side love me too. I tried so hard, only for him to continue looking at me like I was his pet fish or something.

I finally gave up. The two face won the battle and ventured on without me. It wasn't until a few months later that I had heard from a friend about his mom paying him off and how he was amazed he got away with the MPD ordeal. WHO FAKES A SERIOUS DISORDER LIKE THAT?

I wish I could say that I had learned my lesson not to date complete jackasses, but unfortunately, I needed to date one more to pass the test.

When I was 19, I met an adorable young man while volunteering at my cousin's school. He was in the band, knew my family, and had a great way with words... blah blah blah. Keep in mind, meeting him took place about a week before the dreaded Valentine's Day so naturally, I knew I had to move quickly.

Somehow my cousin got it across to him that I had a severe pollen allergy. The man showed up at my house with glass roses, so they wouldn't make me sick. Ugh, so romantic, am I right? He then made me dinner, danced with me in the kitchen, and made me fall for him all in the span of an evening. I fall in love way too quickly.

Once we were exclusive, the little fights started. Bickering is usual in a relationship, but making your girlfriend feel like it's always her fault and she is overly-sensitive is not normal. So I'd break up with him for being a total ass... then I would get back together with him because he always knew what to say. "This time will be different, I promise, I love you." I believed his words so much we even decided to move in together.

My best friend lived in Florida for college, and we would have video chat dates all the time. The issue was that my best friend is a guy, and MY guy didn't handle that very well. Instead of telling me he was jealous, he would shut off the internet so I couldn't get on video chat. He started to tell me who I could and couldn't be friends with and if he felt like I was standoffish he would read all of my text messages.

One day he asked me to marry him, and to my stupidity, I said yes. Not long after that, I found out I was pregnant. I was so excited and felt like my life was falling into place, and that my

20

relationship was only going to become stronger. Then I lost the baby… which was one of the worst days of my life. I took it extremely hard, fell into a self-destructive phase, and eventually tried to end my life. Luckily for me, my best friend was there to stop me from making a huge mistake.

I was sent to treatment for a week and came out knowing that I would never let my life go downhill like that ever again. I decided to leave him, finally. I managed to stay away for a few weeks but then found out I was pregnant again. After telling him, we decided we were going to try and make it work for the baby.

From the moment I was showing, he started accusing me that I had cheated on him and that the baby wasn't his. When she was finally born, I decided for my mental health that it was better if we lived separately. One day I took her over to visit him, and he started to threaten that he wasn't going to give her back to me. Fighting me, he grabbed my neck and chocked me while I was holding our daughter.

I waited too long to end it after that, but I did, and that time, it was for good.

THEN I met the man I was meant to marry. I started as his boss at an Office Depot that we were both working at. He was new, so I asked him to shadow me so he could see how I wanted things done. He didn't have a car, so I also offered to drive him to and from work. On one of the drives, my daughter was in the backseat. When he noticed that the sun was hurting her little eyes, he hopped in the back and covered them, already loving her more than her actual dad.

About a month after he started working with me, I transferred to another store, and he took over my position. I decided to text him and see how everything was going (also because I just wanted a reason to talk to him) and we ended up texting a lot. We finally decided to hang out and ended up talking for hours where then I told him that I didn't want anything serious, especially after the relationship that I had gotten out of.

That all was fine and dandy until I realized that I had fallen completely in love with him. We met on May 18th, 2015, and got married on April 15, 2018. He took on being the world's greatest father to my little girl and later on to our son, who was born this May.

I never knew what I was worth until I met him. Although I had to go through a very toxic relationship to come out where the grass was greener, there were some positives. I had a beautiful daughter with a man who taught me that I have every inch of power to decide how my life goes. I came out of that relationship, stronger, wiser, and so much more appreciative of the man that I am married to now. I deserve the world, and so do you.

* * *

"My only "relationship goal" is someone who motivates me to become a better person and shows me the potential I don't see in myself."

— Jos

Total Control Freak

When we first met, he was married. That should have been red flag number one, but I was young, dumb, and didn't care. Aside from having a wife, he was everything I ever wanted and more. He would take me on expensive dates, pay for everything I wanted, and treated me like a princess.

When came expensive dates, though, came fancy dresses. One night when we went out, he looked at me and told me that he didn't appreciate it when I dressed slutty. His comment completely threw me off, but I slid it under the rug and just never wore that dress again.

Once his divorce was final, we moved in together, and I finally started to notice that things with him weren't exactly healthy. He began to do and say things that would tear me down. One time I was in the shower and he came in, eyed me naked, and told me that he could notice areas that I was gaining weight.

He told me that I needed to start going to the gym at least two days a week until I fixed the issue.

His comments hurt my pride, but he hadn't physically hurt me until about a year and a half into our relationship. He came home one night completely hammered and ready for a fight. He started screaming at me, saying that my car hood was warm, which meant I left the house. I was asleep when he started all the yelling, and I had been home the entire night, so I wasn't sure where all the accusations were coming from.

After denying leaving the house over and over again, we finally went out to my car so we could feel the hood and see if it was warm. He grabbed my arm and held it so tight when we walked outside that I felt my circulation cutting off. When we got to my car, he slammed my face onto the hood to prove his point that it was hot. When I shrieked, he immediately let go and stepped backwards, clearly knowing he was in the wrong. He went on with the "it won't happen again" spiel," but deep down, I knew that it was a lie, and something was seriously wrong with that man.

Not long after that night, he started waking me up in the middle of the night because "it looked like I had a dream about someone else." He then started snatching my phone and going through it even though he never found anything in it. I was beginning to become more and more afraid of him and isolating myself from my friends and family, so that they wouldn't catch on that something was wrong.

I was becoming too skinny from stress and pressure to keep

weight off, too tired from not sleeping, in fear of "dreaming about someone else," and knew that I had to do something before it got worse. I never thought that I would become one of those girls, but I had, and I needed to get out. When I ended it, he threatened to kill himself; so I had to block him, change my number, and move out of town for a little bit. I needed to find myself again after being sucked into such a narcissistic relationship.

It took a long time, and I couldn't have gotten through it without my friends and family; who didn't pass the slightest judgment when I told them all that had happened. After I walked away from him, I felt secure and free. I felt like I was one of the lucky ones who had removed herself from a bad situation before it got worse. I felt like I needed to take all that I knew from it and share it with the world so nobody would make the same mistakes I did.

A couple of years after I left him, I met the man that I'm with now. He has been a dream, and so supportive of my past. There are times when I have a flashback and start to freeze up, but he's always there and notices right away. His love gets me back into reality, and I am so thankful for that.

I want to say that I regret getting into my toxic relationship, but I would never be where I am now if it wasn't for it. I started choosing what made me happy and living the way I wanted life to be. I moved from Georgia to Colorado, and I have never been happier. Hang in there if you're feeling like you're trapped in a bad situation. You got this.

* * *

"I won't beg someone to love me. I learned long ago that there is no use in hopeless pleas of trying to make someone stay. I am too good to chase someone who does not know my worth and I am too wild to keep waiting for some-one who doesn't acknowledge my value. I want to be loved unconditionally. I shouldn't have to fight so hard for it. I do not have the time to prove to someone that I am worth it. I shouldn't have to prove any of that; I am worth more than that."

— *Ming D. Liu, A Story A Day*

Have Some Faith

I prayed for him. I prayed for him every day since I was little. That's what I do, though, I pray. Little did I know that when he was sent to me, he would be one that didn't pray.... and I didn't like that.

A little backstory about me, I'm going to school to get my Masters in Divinity. What does that even mean? You may ask. It means I'm going to school to become a priest of an Episcopal Church. I know, I know, that's so awesome, and I'm already such a strong and independent woman who doesn't need a man. That's very true, but it certainly doesn't mean I don't want one.

I was still in my undergrad when I met my ex. Even then, I knew what I wanted to do with my life but didn't know quite yet what kind of guy I wanted to do it with. My ex was adventurous and loved the outdoors just as much as I did. He made me feel unique and beautiful, and I loved that we had some things in common, until I realized we didn't have the essential elements in common.

When I told him that I wanted to become a priest, all he did was nod like I was speaking in a different language. He blew off my passion like he didn't want to be any part of it. That was red flag number one. When I asked him to come to church with me, he laughed and joked that he couldn't even remember the last time he had gone to church. That was red flag number two.

I'm extremely understanding of those who aren't as serious about their faith as I am, but I do not understand those who judge MY faith. That's what my ex did. Every time I would pray before dinner, go to Church on Sunday, or even talk about my dreams of becoming a Priest, he was judging me. He made it a point to refuse acknowledging how important it all was to me, and that was the final red flag that I needed.

I ended things between us but did it with faith that he just wasn't the right person for me. He taught me a precious lesson. He taught me that my potential partner's faith is a deal-breaker for me. He certainly doesn't have to practice to the level that I do, but supporting my faith and his own is definitely an essential.

I'm thankful for that relationship because I learned more about myself, my goals, and not to ever settle. It was hard to be with someone who made me feel poorly about my passions; but it was easy to let him go because those passions mean more to me than any guy ever could. Heck, I mean more to myself than a guy ever could.

So, my advice to all of you: don't settle just because you think it could work. Don't turn the other cheek when red flags start going up, and don't change who you are just because someone is judging you for it.

Also, make sure your potential partner brushes his teeth and eats his vegetables...that's super important.

* * *

"When you want it the most, there's no easy way out.When you're ready to go, and your heart's left in doubt. Don't give up on your faith, love comes to those who believe it... And that's the way it is."
- Celine Dion

The Project

I was born with this innate need to fix people- family, friends, relationships. You name it. I think this was only heightened by watching my dad's toxic marriage journey with my narcissistic mother. I was verbally and emotionally abused as a child, and I think that, combined with my "fix everyone" mentality is what lead me to some pretty toxic and abusive romantic relationships. My ex-boyfriends had done things like threaten to cheat on me if I didn't sleep with them, or coerce me to have sex with them. However, no one holds a match to my ex-boyfriend Dan.

Dan and I had been friends for years before we began dating. His best friend George was my best friend, and Dan and I lived in neighboring residence halls in college. We ended up on the same trivia team about two summers ago, and that's when it hit me: I liked this guy. Why do you ask? Because he was a project. Dan was quiet, always on his phone, and seemed to be working on setting his future up. I was determined to make this guy fall for me so that I could fix his flaws and make him into the perfect man for me. That should have been a red flag, "Do Not Pass Go," for the average human, but I am not like the average person.

Dan and I slowly began flirting through trivia, and then we started to text and got to know each other better. At the time, I was going on dates with different guys and having a great time playing the field. One of the guys I was going on a date with was Dan and I's mutual friend, Alex. The date with Alex went well, but I knew it was just a one date situation. I informed Dan about my date with Alex, and he texted, "What if I took you out and let you rant about your dating life?" Smooth, man. We set up a time and date for the next week.

Was I interested in Dan as a person? Kind of. Was I interested in getting a chance with this project? You freaking bet.

My first red flag popped up very shortly after he had asked me out. I gave Dan a list of things I enjoyed doing, and guess what? He went with none of them. I brushed it off and told myself that I was determined to have a great time regardless. We ended up going go-karting and then went for coffee. We talked throughout the date, and while I wasn't attracted to him, I was, you guessed it, attracted to his potential.

Our first month of dating was perfect. He treated me well, wanted to spend time with me, and genuinely seemed interested in me. He said he loved me after that month, and I was HOOKED. It seemed that once he knew I was in love with him, though, a switch flipped.

Shortly after, I was accepted into my top graduate school for speech pathology. I was so excited to tell Dan. I sent him the news via text, and all he sent back was "Congrats"…what? That's all you're going to say to your girlfriend after she just received some of the best news of her life? He made no effort to celebrate me or my huge accomplishment, but I decided to brush it off and move along.

He received his Master's degree that May so I got him a thoughtful gift, and wanted to tell the world about his accomplishments. I was over the moon excited that my man had gained a degree in his field of Computer Science.

Things took a turn for the worst when summer hit. He began to find reasons not to see me, never even listened to my love language (words of affirmation), and didn't seem to care about me or my feelings. He would rather hang out at home and do nothing than hang out with me.

I ended things via text because his friends reached out to me and said he had been planning to break up with me, so clearly I had to do it first. He came over to my place right away, which was a first for him (I always had to make the 40-minute drive to see him.) Anyways, he came over, and we talked about our relationship. I expressed all my concerns (there was already a considerable list), and he bursted into tears. I felt guilty for ending it and asked him if he wanted the us to be over. When he replied, "no," I took him back. He was heading to Germany on vacation for the summer, so we agreed to give each other some space and work on things when he got home.

We ended up talking everyday through text, snap chat, and facetime. He was drunk most of the time he was in Germany, and wasted no time in telling me all about it. Around that time, I was starting to develop anxiety. I was in grad school three hours away from my hometown and had no friends at my new school. Combine that with being isolated from a guy who worries you with his drinking, and you've got a mess on your hands.

He returned from Germany three weeks later and made no mention of our relationship. I sat him down a month later, and he told me I had so many things to work on before we could become official again. I had something to work on. ME. The one trying to break her back to make sure he was happy, all while sacrificing my mental health. He then told me that none of his friends liked me. This was a surprise because all of his friends always seemed to include me in all their plans and began to plan events around me being in town. That hurt me so much, so I created time to hang out with all of them one by one in an attempt to gain back their acceptance. It turned out, none of them had any hard feelings toward me at all.

Fasting forward to the Christmas holidays, Dan had no plans to get me anything for until I specifically asked if we were getting each other gifts. Keep in mind; we had been dating off and on for about nine months at that time. Who doesn't get their significant other a gift? Even if that's not your love language, it's still something people do. Common courtesy, man.

He told me that I should also probably get his nieces and nephews gifts too. Did I mention this man only let me meet his family ONCE when we started dating, and then would not let me near them after that?

Dan ended up getting me a beautiful necklace for Christmas, and we moved past that issue. He also began to invite me to more events concerning his friends, starting with a Christmas party. I had plans to wear a nice pair of pants and a sweater until I got a text on the day of the Christmas party telling me precisely what I was required to wear… I'm sorry, but this isn't my first Christmas party. Heaven forbid my man to tell me what I needed to wear. I was anxious and didn't want to start a fight though, so I changed my outfit to what he "required" me to wear.

At the Christmas party, everyone asked who I was. Why? Because my boyfriend didn't bother to introduce me or inform the other people at the Christmas party that he had been dating someone for the past 9 MONTHS. I was crushed, but sucked it up.

New Year's came along, and Dan was my designated driver for the party we had decided to attend. As soon as we got to the party, he started drinking. He told me he had a limit, but after he was way past his limit, I had to step in and remind him that he would not be driving us home drunk. He loudly responded, "Sorry, guess I can't drink anything because the bitch said so"… dude, you're getting drunk when you're the DD is putting our lives in danger… shut up.

That night was the beginning of the end.

Dan woke up the next day and told me he wanted to move to

Germany and had no intention of taking me with him. In his defense, he was born in Germany and moved here when he was three for his dad's job. He missed home and wanted to move back, without me. I broke up with him right then and there for being selfish and not even trying to plan me into his future but then ended up getting back together the next day because he said he would wait until I graduated from graduate school, so I could move with him. I was super anxious about uprooting my life for a guy, but I figured I would eventually be okay so I began learning German and prepared to take on the next semester of graduate school.

By that time, I had officially been diagnosed with anxiety, and Dan wasted no moment to remind me of it. Well, wouldn't you be anxious if you had a boyfriend who didn't include you in anything, told you his friends didn't like you, and always made you the last priority too?

Little by little, Dan made me feel like a huge burden. He never made an effort to drive the three hours to see me while I was away at school, and when I did visit him, he would sit around all weekend and play on his phone. I finally sat him down and told him how to treat me and this relationship even though I knew he didn't care about me. I wasn't strong enough to leave him yet but that all changed the day before my 24th birthday.

February 15th was a perfect day. Dan and I decided to celebrate Valentine's Day a day late, as I was in town for that weekend. He took me out to a nice dinner, actually complimented how I was dressed, and was a complete gentleman. We both went to sleep that night very, very happy.

The next day, Dan decided to take me on a tour of Nebraska Furniture Mart because I had never been. As we walked through the store, I began to make a bunch of puns as I usually did when we hung out. At one point, he got upset with me, and I got quiet. When we got home, he went into his room and refused to talk to me. I walked in three separate times, asking him to communicate with me before my birthday party that night, but he wouldn't.

When we finally spoke, we only had an hour to get ready for my party. Did I mention that I planned everything for my birthday party? Did I also mention that Dan didn't even tell me he was coming to my birthday until I confirmed with him a couple of days before? Moving along.

Dan decided to get food right before we had to leave for my party and came back very, very late. At that point, I was frustrated because HE was making me late for MY birthday. I explained why I was upset and that we were going to be late, but it would all be okay. He got furious, called me a "fucking princess" and told me to "fuck off."

As we continued to walk, he hit me with his bag of food. I was crushed and terrified of him. When we got to his place, I began to get changed, and he threw a blanket at me. I walked over to him and told him he could talk to me like an adult instead of throwing things, and he got up, put his hands on me, and pushed me into the wall of his living room. At that point, I knew I had to get out. I called my dad, who rushed to get me, and told me to lock myself in a room until he got there. As soon as I got the text that he was there, I ran as fast as I could out of

Dan's apartment, blocked him on every social media platform I could think of, and never looked back.

My abusive relationship ended that day. It took being physically abused to see what my friends and family saw. I had learned that his ex had also blocked him on every social media platform, leading me to believe that something similar had happened to her. I began my healing process as soon as I could. I threw myself into school, got on medication for my anxiety, started running, and started going back to church.

Little by little, things got better. I put on the ten pounds I had lost while dating Dan, got back into my favorite hobby-running, and I got my sanity back. I still have a long road to go, but after seven months of therapy and support, I now know that I don't deserve to date projects. I'm a queen who deserves my king, and so are you.

* * *

"Work on being in love with the person in the mirror who has been through so much but is still standing."

Codependent

T he best way to describe my past relationship is "codependent." Both of us were struggling with mental health problems when we started dating, but mine was forced to the sidelines so I could help him with his. There were nights that I stayed up until four in the morning, trying to talk him through an anxiety attack. He refused to go and get help and continuously told me that it would make me a terrible girlfriend if I didn't help him.

As an independent woman, I moved into my very first apartment during my last year of college. Without discussing living together, he decided to move himself in as well, even though he had a place of his own. To make matters worse, he started pointing out that I hadn't dusted or cleaned in a while. The pressure of taking care of him, living with him, and making sure I wasn't going to be judged started to drain me emotionally. No matter how hard I tried to push him away and make plans that didn't include him, he would not leave me alone.

During the Spring semester, my mental health was at its lowest, and I attempted suicide. He walked in on my attempt, forced me to stop, and left it at that. He never asked me if I was okay afterwards and never did anything to try and get me the help that I needed. He got one of his friends to talk to me instead of being a man and talking to me himself. She even agreed that it was weird.

By the summertime, I had moved back home. It was then that I realized how much easier it was to breathe and feel content without him around. I broke up with him soon after that, and of course, it took him over a month to come close to accepting it. Even then, I ended up having to block him on everything because when he wasn't able to get in touch with me, he started trying to get to me through my mom. He thought that since I hadn't deleted the pictures of us off of social media, that there was still hope. I never realized how difficult it was to be with someone who latches on and doesn't know how to let go.

That relationship, in addition to my existing mental health issues, caused me to need hospitalization. I spent a week in-patient and continued onto an out-patient facility for two months. Both of those great therapeutic times helped me to find my peace. It helped me find my comfort with everything that was going on around me, and inside of me. I released a lot of anger and let go of people that I knew I couldn't have around if I wanted to keep my new found peace.

It wasn't a quick recovery in the slightest, but it was the best thing I ever did for myself. I have always been one to care about others more than myself, and being in a codependent relationship taught me that I should always come first in my life. Now I have the strength to work through whatever is thrown at me, and I also have a wonderful fiance who opened up space in his heart to accept me for who I am and allow me to continue healing.

I suppose one of the biggest things I learned during that hard time in my life is that there are certain things to wait for, but waiting for a time to take care of yourself is not one of them.

* * *

"We are all broken, that's how the light gets in."
— Ernest Hemingway

Cinco De Bye(o)

"*S*he's just a friend" is one of the hardest statements to believe when it's coming out of your boyfriend's mouth. Yet, that was his reply when I asked him about a girl he had been spending a lot of time with. They texted all the time and hung out one on one.. but she was just a friend. Bullshit.

He was my first boyfriend and would have been my first love if he wasn't so emotionally abusive. He was always putting me down and making me feel crazy or stupid for asking simple questions. For example, I was a psycho for asking him about the girl who was "just his friend."

When we were around others, though, he was an angel. He was polite, caring, and seemed like he was all over the best guy around. He had everyone fooled… except for me, who had to deal with the abuse when we got home.

He finally showed his true colors to the public when he broke up with me and left me to be with the "friend" I was crazy for questioning him about. Not to mention he decided to do all of that after I had major surgery and needed all the care I could get — some angel.

Now he is an actual angel. He passed away last Cinco De Mayo, quite suddenly. Of course, that made it extremely hard to think poorly of him, but at the end of the day, he wasn't kind to me. It took me until recently to truly get over his death, but I like to think I had some help.

I met a guy that not only treats me as his equal, but respects me, communicates with me, and certainly doesn't abuse me verbally. My ex, rest his soul, taught me how a boyfriend was not supposed to act and to wait until I find someone who I deserved. I have hope that the girl he left me for also realized that she deserved better. She deserves a man who doesn't hide her and who doesn't have a girlfriend while they are sneaking around.

The good news is that even when things fall apart and seem like they are at the lowest, it always and I mean ALWAYS gets put back together. I, and so many others out there are proof.

Rest in peace, ex-boyfriend.

* * *

"So what if he doesn't love you anymore. You didn't have him in your life once before and you were fine. So you'll be fine without him again. All you need to do now is show him that it was his loss,

Cinco De Bye(e)

not yours."

Made A Job Of It

*D*id you know that a boyfriend can psychically abuse you without even living together? I do now. How do I know? Because I went through it in high school.

Most of my peers in high school dated someone for like two months and then called it quits, with no questions asked. My relationship was much different, against my own will. I would have called it quits after a couple of months, but I literally couldn't.

When I started dating him, I never thought of him as someone who would hit anyone, much less a female…but I was way off. During our very first fight, he didn't just hit me… he beat the crap out of me. That was all it took to know that I needed to end it and get out of there as soon as I could, so I broke up with him. Unfortunately for me, breaking up with him landed me with bruises, sexual assault, and a relationship that I was stuck in.

I was so afraid to get hurt again that I stayed in the relationship way longer than I should have. I was genuinely fearful of what he would do if I tried to end it again, knowing that bI would be walking away from someone who wanted to hurt me ,and wasn't going to stop until he did. That seemed much less ideal than just sucking it up and pretending to be the perfect couple.

When I finally got up the courage to tell someone about what I had been dealing with, they helped me get a protective order. I was able to end my relationship and know that he legally could not come near me. It was the most comforting feeling in the entire world, and I am so glad that I spoke up about it.

I'm 23 now and working with families who are experiencing child abuse. Although what I went through was terrible, it lead me to my passion for helping teens and young kids who are dealing with what I did, and worse. When I help a family, I feel like I have come full circle. I take all of the anger and pain that I have from that relationship, and I put it towards helping others cope and understand that they aren't alone or hopeless.

If you are in a situation like that or know someone who is, please don't wait to take legal action. There are people out there that can help you and keep you safe. I'm one of those people and I am finally safe.

* * *

"Someday you're gonna look back on this moment of your life as such a sweet time of grieving. You'll see that you were in mourning and your heart was broken, but your life was changing..."

Girlfriend's Guide To Heartbreak

— *Elizabeth Gilbert*

Pressure

When I was in high school, I started dating my first ever boyfriend. I thought of him as everyone thinks about their first love. I thought I was going to marry him, have his babies, and live happily ever after.

That was until things took a severe turn.

Every little thing I did started to be wrong. What I wore, who I hung out with, and most of the other decisions I made that didn't even have to do with him. If I chose to go out with my friends instead of stay in with him, it would lead to an instant fight. When I decided not to go and see him because my grandmother had flown in from California to see us, he went off on me. He didn't yell at me in private either; he made his anger very public and super embarrassing.

I let him get mad at me because I thought that was part of being in a relationship. I had always been told that "love" was work,

47

and you have to work for it regardless if you feel it. I figured my relationship issues were the same as everyone else's.

Aside from the anger, he made me do sexual things that I didn't know how to do, and didn't WANT to do. I was so uncomfortable but I was afraid to speak up. He told me that if I loved him, I would do it. I wanted to save those things for my future husband, but I let pressure ruin that for me.

It wasn't until I graduated from high school that I realized I didn't want to live like that anymore. I spent two years being bullied, abused and pressured by a guy that I didn't love. He constantly berated and belittled me just for existing, and that wasn't fair; so I ended it and immediately felt the weight of an elephant was lifted off of my shoulders.

It was past time and honestly the right timing because I was planning to go off to college during the Fall. I was able to start fresh and leave the toxic relationship behind. I felt lost at the beginning, after being with someone for two years and being on my own for the very first time. I struggled with severe anxiety and depression. I continually felt angry with myself that I let someone treat me the way he did.

I genuinely think I coped better because I was in a new place and began to reinvent who I was. Even on the worst days, I got up, went to class, exercised, and socialized to the best of my ability. I made wonderful friends who supported me through my grieving stages, and I even met the love of my life whom I plan to marry. From then on, I made a promise to continue to do things for myself and not feel the guilt to explain who I am to anyone. That is a promise I will never break and a promise that every one should make to themselves.

* * *

"When you go through a negative situation, don't think about it. Make it positive."

- Yoko Ono

"We Can Make It Through Anything"

*L*et's start with the background. I left home to move 313 miles away for college which was my first time leaving home for a long period of time. I grew up in the same house my entire life. When I got to college, I was fortunate enough to meet some fantastic people who I quickly became friends with. We would all hang out in the pool room playing cards, studying, shooting pool, and that's where I met him.

He was a big goofball, full of energy, and he had this way of making everyone he met love him. The man quickly became my best friend. We were always together. After school, we would watch movies, go for long drives, play pool, talk about music, and talk about life. He meant so much to me already; it felt like I had known him my entire life. I am a very oblivious person, though, who thought that all he wanted was a friendship… until he was drunk.

We were pre-gaming for a big bonfire at our friend's house

and he was drinking more heavily than usual. I figured he just needed to release some stress but little did I know, he was trying to get the courage to tell me how he felt.

Fast forward to the party, and we were sitting in his Jeep, having a heart to heart when he finally confessed his love for me. It took me back for a second, seeing that I never thought he'd ever feel that way about me. I pondered the thought for a few days, trying to decipher my feelings for him but then I finally concluded that I did actually like him too, a lot.

I'm not the type of person who gets into relationships or attaches to others, so it meant a lot for me to believe I had feelings for someone else. On a drive around town late at night, we decided to stop at the park down the way. I started joking around with him, feeling nervous at the newfound attraction. After some awkward conversations, I decided that something needed to be done, so I kissed him and quickly apologized after. That's where the adventure began.

Fast forward a few weeks, and we went on our first official date. He took me to a steakhouse, and then we drove to the top of a mountain, where we looked out into our small town, taking in all the lights and stars. That's where he officially asked me to be his girlfriend.

Things were going great after that. We spent a lot of time together and never got tired of each other. Soon enough, we fell deeper and deeper in love. We even met each other's families and visited each other's home states.

51

The trouble didn't start until the day of graduation. He was from New Jersey, and I was from Michigan. We were both in college in Pennsylvania, but didn't plan to stay there. We decided that our love could handle the long distance and knew that we would close the gap eventually, but we both had some things that we needed to take care of back home first. So every few months one of us would fly to the other for a weekend. We were making it work well; video chatting all the time and talking on the phone before bed almost every night. The love was still going strong... at least for one of us.

At that point, it had been around two years that we had been together. He started to act funny, and my anxiety had been high. He reassured me numerous times that everything was okay, but I couldn't shake the feeling. I asked him if we could watch our show together after he got off of work, and he agreed but ended up spending the entire night driving around. That's when I knew for sure that something was up.

I was right... that was the end. He told me that he couldn't handle the distance anymore, that it was too difficult for him. I begged him to stay., reminding him that we said we could make it through anything and that the distance was only temporary. He seemed unsure and said he needed a few days to think about everything. At that point, I was a wreck. Tears were running down my face, I couldn't breathe and could barely talk.

My roommate tried to console me, but nothing helped. I couldn't move. I was broken inside and out and felt as if my heart had been ripped out of my chest, and laid out on the table in front of me. Everything was dark and bleak. I tried to go to work the next day but had to leave to come home. My life felt like it was over. I could barely eat, I didn't want to see any friends, and I couldn't even sleep in my bed. I spent weeks on the couch.

He said that he would think about things, but I knew it was over. I also knew the reason he gave me was a partial lie. There was another girl, even though he told me I had nothing to worry about since she had a kid, knowing that he didn't want children yet. "I don't want baby daddy drama, she's only a friend," he would say to me to try and calm me down, but I had a horrible gut feeling, which I can now confirm.

It was over, done, and there was nothing I could do to change his mind. I gave him his time, gave him his space and even told him my plan to close the distance. I told him how I felt and that I didn't want to lose him. He was the only person I ever saw an actual future with. He was so good to me, so good with me and I didn't know how in the hell I could ever get over it.

It took weeks, possibly months, until I finally let my friends come over. I had completely lost track of all time. I felt terrible because I was just a ball of grief sitting in the corner. I was no fun to be around and all I wanted to do is cry and sleep; but my friends still wanted to be by my side. They knew I'm wasn't good at processing emotions, but slowly I started to feel a bit of happiness again. I began to be able to smile and laugh again.

I deleted everything of his off of my phone; his number, our texts, all photos of us, and things that we did together, so I couldn't look at them as easily. He had blocked me on all forms of social media a few days after things ended, so I couldn't see anything he was doing, and yes, I did try to check.

The pain stuck around for so long that I couldn't even try to talk to another man without feeling like I was cheating. That feeling lasted for months.

It's been almost a year now since things ended, and I can finally say that I have moved on. I can look at old photos of us and not feel my heart drop. Instead I enjoy the memories of being happy then. I can listen to music that reminds me of him and not have to turn it off. I can smile and enjoy life, and very importantly, I can go on dates and not feel guilt. I can live my life again and be myself.

It took about three months to sleep in my bed again, four months to listen to music again, and about two months to form even a small smile. Finally, it took a year to be able to say that I think I have moved on. I used to get so angry when someone would tell me that with time it would get better, but they were telling the truth. It may not feel like it, but time helps. Time, and wonderful friends!

* * *

"Now is the time to regroup and pamper yourself. Find the small things that make you happy, such as lunch with friends or reading a good book and indulging yourself."

Just My Roommate?

I met my ex in August of 2015. Amazingly, we grew up in the same town but had never crossed paths until I downloaded the popular app, Tinder. We ended up falling in love faster than I swiped right on him.

When we met, I had just come out of a seven-year-long abusive relationship, and he was enjoying the dating spree life, aka sleeping around. My toxic relationship became such a thing in the past once he came into the picture, and he dropped every girl he had been talking to because he didn't want anyone else but me.

We had the absolute best times together. After two years of dating, we bought a house and adopted a dog. We were a little family that had it all, including a fight-less relationship. Who would have thought not fighting with your partner would end up being a problem…

Work decided to separate us for a little bit, and it wasn't until that time apart that I realized we had become complacent and comfortable. Those are two words that should never be used to describe a relationship: red flag, red flag.

I have a super emotionally draining tax job, and when I would come home on edge, he was nowhere to be found with support or love. He could give two craps when I talked about my day with him, so I ended up just stopping, and he continued to detach emotionally.

When we first met, we both admitted how attracted we were to not being overly emotional or needy. That was still the case, but I had been asking for support, and even then, he couldn't seem to give it to me. He was supposed to be there to pick me up when I was down and talk me off of a ledge, always. That was gone, though. So one morning, I rolled over in bed, told him I was unhappy, and moved out.

Making that decision sounds easy on paper, but in reality, it was one of the toughest things I had to do. He was my best friend and would still be if we had just left our relationship at that. We were so good at being roommates, terrific at having fun together, but extremely bad at intimacy and thinking about our future as a couple.

I feel like these situations happen much more than we realize, and that's one of the reasons I wanted to put my story into this book. He and I were so wrapped up on finding our soulmates that we looked past the risks and reasoning behind it all. We got impatient when it came to finding a life partner and forgot that best friends could also be life partners, just without the romance.

I wish every day that our friendship didn't end the way it did, but I am also so thankful for the experience because it taught me to be patient and wait for real love to come around. I know it's going to someday, so now all I can do is sit back and live MY life to the fullest.

* * *

"One of the happiest moments ever, is when you find the courage to let go of what you can't change."

Love On A Cruise Ship

I met him on cruise way back in 2008; yeah yeah, I know, a Hallmark movie waiting to happen. I was fourteen, and he had just turned sixteen. he was an older man with long legs, awkward floppy brown hair, and bright blue eyes that I swear matched the ocean. We spent most of our three days on the cruise together, and it did not take me long to fall for him (or at least think I had.)

When we got off of the cruise ship, we exchanged our Facebook accounts and added each other immediately. Although he didn't live where I did, he went to the same college as my brother, which seemed pretty convenient, even though I only ended up seeing him twice.

The first time I visited, we went on a semi-date, which consisted of us making out in his car and telling each other how we wished we lived closer. After that somewhat date, I could have sworn that he was the one I was going to marry. Not a minute went by that I didn't think about him or replay the memories of kissing him in my head.

The second time I visited him was a couple of months later, and it felt like things changed for the worst between us. Instead of forming bad memories though, I decided to keep the good ones and go on with my life.

When I finally graduated high school, I decided to go out of state for college. Not even a month into my freshman year, I found out that my teenage love was getting married. To this day, I can still feel the pain in my heart; feeling like it was being ripped out of my chest. Thinking of him marrying someone other than me sent me through a whirlwind of depression and loneliness. It took longer than it should have for me to realize that I wasn't in love with him, but I was in love with the idea of him.

Six years later, I left Florida where I had been working, and headed back to Houston, Texas, where my parents were living. I had always dreamed of joining the Navy, so when I got settled in Texas, that is what I did. It was the big step I needed to feel like I knew who I was, and what I was supposed to do. I was so happy with where I was in my life that I decided I had nothing to lose by reaching out to my long lost teenage love.

To my surprise, he replied quickly. It turned out that he had gotten divorced and asked me to meet up. Seeing him brought me back and made me feel like no time had passed since we last saw each other. All of my feelings for him flooded back without me having any say in the matter. He seemed to feel the same way about me but was able to reel the emotions back in much quicker.

He was in flight school and made it very clear that he didn't want a long-distance relationship. He got divorced because his ex-wife had cheated on him when he was gone, and he just wasn't ready to risk that again, which I completely understood. The difference between that time and when he was in college, though? I wasn't dumb enough to walk away and pretend like he didn't exist. I decided to wait until it was our time to be together.

That's what I'm doing to this day, but in the healthiest way I can. Although I dream of the day that he wants me for good, I refuse to stop living my life the way I want, and continue to work towards my career in the Navy. It may seem like my story isn't about overcoming heartbreak, but let me tell you, not being able to be with the person you love when you know they love you too, is heartbreak on its own.

It's okay, though, because I am who I want to be with or without him; and if the day comes where we can take the next step, I won't be leaving myself behind.

* * *

"Time is the best teacher; patience is the best lesson"

—*e boah*

The Boy Next Door

*S*o there was this guy who lived next door to me. His name was, well, for the safety of this identity and mine; let's name him Jeremy. I was pretty sure he was my soulmate. How did the story actually go though…? Well, I'll tell you.

I had noticed that I had a new neighbor right next door, and it happened to be this attractive guy. What I knew of him was that he had a dog and drove a truck. We had a couple of interactions here and there, but nothing worth mentioning. On Friday the 6th (yes, I remember the date) I heard a knock at the door and low and behold it was him. He was delivering my mail to me, and we ended up talking for quite some time. He had told me his name, and I certainly remembered it! Note: This is very unusual behavior for me. I never remember anyone's name.

A few days passed, and we happened to be on our balconies at the same time. Again we struck up a conversation, a long one, I might add. Somewhere in between my rambling, I mentioned how many bottles of wine I had just purchased. Jeremy took that as an invitation to come over and suddenly I heard a knock at the door. It was Jeremy with a bottle of wine in his hand! We continued talking for ages until it was just about midnight, and he had to leave.

The next day I was on my balcony, anxiously waiting to see Jeremy again. I was too nervous to knock on his door and make my presence known, so I waited on my balcony. He finally came out with his dog, and we both acknowledged each other. At that point, I was nervous and didn't know what to say. Dear Lord, did that bite me in the ass because he thought he did something wrong with me to entice such behavior. I didn't know what to say! I knew I liked the kid, but I get nervous sometimes.

Anyway, the next day, we talked once again from our balconies, and I must say I looked so cute that day and Jeremy asked for my number. About time!

.Jeremy and I had been inseparable since we met. In between texting all day, we finally went on our first date, and that was the first time he kissed me. This now brings me to Thursday, October 19th, 2017. That day was actual perfection. It was close to sunset, and the evening was beautiful! We both hurried to get ready and then drove to the lake to watch the sunset. There was some music off in the distance that set the mood as we just sat and looked up at the stars. We talked, shared jokes, shared fun facts, and even picked out the different star formations. At one point, he was lying on my legs as I was rubbing my hands through his hair. At that moment, I knew he meant more to me than anyone ever in my life. I thought

I might marry him and wouldn't mind at all. He made me so happy and experience pure bliss.

That night was the night I fell in love with him.

Then January 28th came around, when he dumped me. Wait; what? I'm sure that's what you just said reading this. By all means, I was just as shocked as you were. What had happened that lead to a breakup? I would like to know, as well. All I know is that it happened, and it was the absolute worst. I couldn't stop thinking about him. I couldn't stop wishing I could be kissing and hugging him.

Enough of that bullshit, listen to this, ready? Well, the Sunday after our breakup, Jeremy was a dick over a snap chat group. Why he does this, I have no idea. So naturally, I decided to call him out on being such an ass. Well, this lead to almost hooking up with him. Wait; what? I know you're probably thinking, "yikes" and "run girl!" Love does some weird things to you. I yelled, we wrestled, and we kissed each other. At one point, he had me pinned me up to his wall, whispering in my ear and pressing his lips to my neck.

Ultimately, we are each other's kryptonite.

This part is going to sound silly, but I prayed to God, saying, "If he's the right one and loves me, make him knock on my window." Low and behold, there was a slap, yes, an actual slap, on the window. I screamed because it scared me! I jumped up and ran outside, only to see it was silent and empty. I walked around for a good ten minutes, wondering where Jeremy was.

Suddenly, I saw him, and he started smiling. He walked to check his mail, trying to avoid me. That's when I called him out, and of course, he denied it completely. I asked him several times why he was smiling, and he was told me it was because I was smiling and that my smile is contagious. Thus, began an hour and half of hanging out, wrestling, and laughing.

Eventually, I ended up leaving, but before I did, he gave me a big hug and said, "I'm so sorry for being an asshole sometimes. It just happens." He did apologize earlier in the night for being rude as well and I appreciated him apologizing to me, but honestly I just enjoyed hanging out with him. About a week after that, I hadn't heard a word so I texted him that I wanted my things back, and no longer wanted anything to do with him. My question was though, did he still want something to do with me?

Fast forward a couple more weeks. I was sitting on my balcony, and Jeremy came out with his dog. We flirted like we usually did when seeing each other, and then he went back inside. I knew I had to know the feelings I felt for him but it was always going to be a tease between us. It was only me making an effort and reaching out towards him. My heart hurt, and my soul completely felt lost.

Then, Jeremy moved out.

That was the end of an era. He had a girl living with him, and they're still living together as far as I know. He's dangled her throughout his Instagram and snap chat and honestly, she came out of the woodwork. Anyways though, he no longer lived next to me.

How did that make me feel? It made me feel weird and extremely empty. I wished that he would come back, knock on my door, and tell me goodbye the right way. I didn't want his last words to be "have a good life." I wanted him to be with me one last time. I wanted to hold in him my arms and hear him breathe as he slept. I wanted to breathe in his smells and feel his energy as he lied next to me in my bed. I wanted to kiss him one last time and wanted to hear his voice again.

I know all good things must come to an end, but I wanted my end, my proper end. Where we both hug and shake on the fact that we are living separate lives. He changed my world, and he has yet to know the real feelings I had for him. Whether or not his feelings were real, mine were, 100%. He got what he wanted from me and left. He robbed me of my soul, and I'll never get that part back again. Of course, I don't hate him for it since it was his to take after all; I just wanted one proper goodbye. Now he has moved out though. There is no more. That was his goodbye.

He got engaged over New Year's after seeing the girl for nearly five months. Then he eloped randomly without telling anyone.

It took a little while to fill the empty feeling in my heart, but I did. I stepped back and realized that our relationship caused much more hurt than happiness, and became thankful that he walked away... well, moved away, but still.

I guess now you're waiting for the moral of the story... – don't date your neighbor.

* * *

"Don't throw stones at your neighbors, if your own windows are glass"

- Benjamin Franklin

Sharing My Best Friend

꧁꧂

At the end of college, I finally started dating the guy that I had been in love with for eight years. We had been excellent friends, and he finally admitted that he knew he loved me too, and had for the past five years. Graduating from college and getting my dream guy made me feel like my life was falling together perfectly.

After a year of dating, I bought a house and asked him to move in with me: significant steps, man. Unfortunately, a few months later, he lost his job, and I stepped up to pay all of his bills, because he was overly stressed about having no income and no savings. It sounds normal until I explain that he had no savings, because he spent them all to build a new computer that he could play video games on.

There he was, no job, no money and no motivation to do anything but sleep and play video games all day. Meanwhile, I was working my booty off, and coming home every day to make dinner, clean the house and pay bills. There were so many days that I had asked him to do his laundry or the dishes while I was at work, but he never got around to doing them, not once.

Instead of asking him to do housework, I decided to try and encourage him to look for jobs and go in for interviews. Did he do that? Of course not. Why do that when you can sit on your ass and play video games. So, I kept moving forward and found him a program that allowed him to take classes on his own time, and become certified in the field he was interested in. The only downside was that he was working, taking classes, and making time for video games, which meant I hardly got to see him.

Time went by and he was very dedicated to his program and also seemed even more dedicated to me, telling our friends and me that he was going to propose soon. I was so giddy for him to pop the question that I could hardly contain my impatience. He claimed that he was going to propose when he felt like he had enough money, which made sense... until he bought himself a six hundred dollar drone... while I still paid all of the bills...

A little farther down the line, I would come home super excited to see him, and he would jerk away from me immediately. My friends were starting to comment that it seemed like I was begging for love and giving him everything, only to receive nothing in return. I defended him and told them that he was just busy getting his life going; but I soon found out that defending him was the worst thing I could have done.

He had been cheating on me, and then lied to me when I

confronted him about it… even though I caught him in the lie over and over again. He was so cold and unrecognizable by then that I finally snapped and kicked him out for good. I hoped that he would be miserable and lost without me, but instead, he told his friends that he found joy watching me cry over him. Who the heck finds joy in others' pain?

A few months after our dramatic breakup, I was playing Ariel from The Little Mermaid and had all of my friends coming to opening night to support me. ALMOST all of my friends, that is. Right before it was my turn to hit the stage, I got a text from my best friend of twelve years. I figured it was going to be a sweet "break a leg" text, but instead, she felt the need to text me that she was dating my cheating, using, good for nothing ex-boyfriend.

I cried more tears over that than I ever thought I could. Nine months after I got that glorious text, they were engaged and moved to another state. After years of excuses, when I asked him about proposing, he went and married my best friend in less than a year of dating. My heart was broken.

I lost my best friend, my boyfriend, her family who I thought of as my own, his family who I was incredibly close to, and a future that I thought I had in the palm of my hand. I felt like I was living in a nightmare that I couldn't wake up from. I was so alone and lost in my life, and honestly didn't see myself being okay again… but I was.

I took the step to start seeing a therapist and reached out to friends who were there through the whole process, with shoulders to cry on. With both of those support systems, I was able to come out stronger in time. Now, I am thankful for those events because I would have probably stayed and been miserable with my ex, and I wouldn't have met the man I see now.

I also wouldn't have a juicy story to tell you all for this book, so you can say I'm thankful for that as well. YOU. WILL. BE. OKAY. AGAIN.

I promise.

* * *

"If she glows after the breakup, you were the problem."

Comfort Zone

◄──◦∞◦──►

I think we can all agree that our first-ever relationships are the ones that pull us in and hurt the most. At least that's how mine was.

I dated the same guy on and off throughout high school. He was my first real boyfriend but became more of a comfort zone than a boyfriend throughout the years; especially my senior year of high school. I clung on to him so tight that year because I was terrified of all the change that was going to happen. I planned to graduate, move to a new city, and wait for him to finish high school (since he was a year younger.)

Near the end of my senior year, I was sexually assaulted by one of my boyfriend's friends, and that changed everything for me. This happened in my neighborhood, which made it feel like it was no longer safe or comfortable. I also started to feel uncomfortable with my boyfriend, with little reminders about what his friend did whenever he would try and touch me, even when it was just a hug. He knew something had happened but didn't know what, and I had decided not to tell him, in fear of what he would do.

I had so much love for my boyfriend, but I couldn't get past the traumatic events and felt myself falling out of love with him very quickly. I didn't just fall out of love with him, though, I also fell out of love with myself. I felt like a completely different person; but I still stayed with him, even though it was merely for comfort.

I needed change and needed it sooner rather than later; so I decided to take a big step out of my comfort zone and cut my hair short. My hair had been long my entire life up until then, but I no longer liked the way I felt with it. That change helped a little, but not enough. I needed to get out of the town I was living in sooner than I had planned to.

I traveled the entire summer and slowly felt like I was beginning to be myself again, which felt amazing. I felt like I was physically growing back into a person. My boyfriend was incredibly supportive through all of my traveling, but when I got back, the love I had for him was still gone. I knew I had to end it, even though it was going to be one of the most robust changes to get over.

Our breakup was much different than most I experienced because it was a whole other type of heartbreak. I wasn't just grieving my first relationship, but I was also grieving the person I used to be before I was assaulted. It hurt so much to leave him, but I knew it wasn't fair to stay just because I needed comfort and was afraid to be alone. I needed to learn that I was going to be okay alone and that when I was ready, someone would come along and accept me for all of my painful past.

I think people must understand that they do not have to stay in a relationship just because it's comfortable. The person you are with doesn't deserve it, and neither do you. It's so incredibly hard to leave your comfort zone and your first relationship; because you associate that relationship with who you were before life got complicated.

Although stepping out of your comfort zone is scary, there are so many beautiful things outside of it and I highly suggest you find out for yourselves.

* * *

"Never be afraid to fall apart because it is an opportunity to rebuild yourself the way you wish you had been all along."

— Rae Smith

7 Years

My ex and I were together for about seven years. We started dating in high school when we were both 15. I was a freshman, and he was a sophomore. I had come into high school, having lost 60 pounds in 3 months (always the big girl), but still didn't feel good about myself. I thought high school was going to suck, and no boys would want to talk to me even though I had lost a bunch of weight.

My ex added me on Facebook two weeks before school started, and I didn't know him, but it said he went to the same high school, so I figured why not? I added him, and nothing came of it at first. Then the first week of high school went by, and he messaged me, "hi." I said "Hey! What's up?" and that started seven years down the rabbit hole of our relationship (two years were fun, the rest was hell for me.)

He had confided in me with a giant secret within the first five minutes of us talking. I asked him why he told me and he said that he had a strong feeling to tell me. He told me that he had intrusive thoughts, OCD; meaning that is head would tell him things that weren't true, and he knew that, but it wouldn't go away, and he'd start believing it.

When we started dating the FIRST time, he was super sweet, but wouldn't even acknowledge me in front of his friends. Red flag #1. I should also say that the first time I went to his house, he forced me to give him a BJ. I said I didn't feel comfortable with it, and he said, "it's fine, it's easy just go." I was hesitant, but he pulled his man part out, and I started going towards it before he pushed my head down very hard. When he was about to finish, I told him not to do it in my mouth, and it turned into an argument. He was very, very upset with me for days, and acted like it was all my fault — red flag #2.

Three weeks later, he ended up breaking up with me over the phone because his friends told him to because I was "a giant ape." It happened while we were both at our high school football game (which he told me he wasn't coming to.) —Red flag #3.

I got over it and talked to other guys, but then we started talking again a few months later. I always had this feeling of not wanting to be away from him and liked him a lot despite the bullshit he did. We started "dating" again, and that lasted two weeks before I broke up with him, because he said he didn't like my friends.

At the end of my freshman year, we talked again and ended up dating for the THIRD time. The first two years were good (in my head) other than the fact that he hated my friends, blamed everything on his OCD, and I mean EVERYTHING (red flag #4 at least.) Again, I say it was good because we did have a lot of amazing and fun memories together, just not all the time.

THEN the accusations started. I always felt guilty when he would say things like "my head is telling me you fucked up/I don't love you/etc." I knew it was his disease and he couldn't control it, but it started to feel like he just used it as an excuse. The moment everything started going downhill (very slowly over the next four years.....) was the time he turned to me and said, "well, you're cheating on me because my head says so." Boom. There was my first turning point.

Our whole relationship revolved around his OCD and I tried to seperate that from our relationship, but it was impossible. I distanced myself from all my friends, and a few of them resented me for a long time. Lots of friends told me I was being stupid (I was) and listed all of the things wrong, while giving examples. I loved him though and honestly didn't want to see or believe it even though I knew it was there.

He went off to college about 30 minutes away when I was a senior in college. I went up to stay with him every weekend right after school; because he refused to come to my place. We then lost our virginity to each other, and for a little while, things got a bit better. We weren't fighting as much, the accusations died down, and it was lovely. Later, I realized it was because we weren't around each other 24/7 anymore and didn't have to interact.

Then I went to the same college as him. I wanted to go to this college regardless if he went or not; while he went because I wanted to go. He had a dorm and I had a dorm, but he NEVER stayed at his. He was at my dorm 24/7. Since were in the same place finally, he didn't want me out of his sight. Any new person I met (especially guys) were questioned and it made me very unhappy. I acted like nothing was wrong around everyone else, but I had never been so miserable in my life.

Why did I stay? Because I was comfortable, in love, and thought things would get better. What a great excuse… be emotionally abused and controlled only to appear like I was happy and in a cute "high school sweetheart" story. We had talked about kids and life and marriage, and honestly, there were times where I was terrified that was actually going to happen. Then we got a dog together. WOO DOGS AND KIDS FIX EVERYTHING, RIGHT?

I paid for 80% of everything, and she is my dog. Fast forward to the summer of 2017; I got accepted to go to a study abroad program for my major and got to travel around Europe for two weeks. It was so much fun, definitely one of the best trips of my life. At that point, my ex and I had seen each other maybe twice within two months before my trip. We texted a lot, but "texting was boring," so if anything, that was the end of the relationship for the most part.

During part of my trip, when I was in Switzerland on the top of Mount Titlis, I looked out over the horizon and started crying. It had finally hit me…. that was the first time in SEVEN YEARS that I had been genuinely happy without a worry in the world.

THAT was my realization after seven years of my friends and family telling me how bad it was, how much my life sucked, and how miserable I had been.

I got back to the states, and we talked maybe three times before the inevitable happened. I got a text that said, "I'm ending this relationship. I need to move on. I need to go," and then silence. He unfriended me on everything and denied any sense of real closure.

To this day, I hate HOW it ended, not THAT it ended. I wish he could have been a bit more of an adult and had a face-to-face conversation. I'll admit it; I called him 40 times, and cried because yes, I was happy it was ending, but I was also a bit scared. Seven years to get comfortable and in 3 sentences, it was officially over. I was super scared. Who would love me? Who would care about me again? Would I ever find someone? I loved this man for so long and POOF.

Here's the "hindsight is 20/20" part. I was in love with my first relationship. I was in love with the perfect story I had created in my head. I was comfortable with being miserable and it had become my lifestyle. I never really loved him; I was just in love with the idea of it all.

It broke my heart to hear the things he said to and about me, broke my heart to disappoint him, but it mostly broke my heart to know that I let it go on for so long. People say, "oh, it's not your fault! Don't blame yourself! It's not women's fault not to leave!" but there was never any physical fear of leaving; he would never have physically hurt me, and I shouldn't have stayed so long to be comfortable, while I was miserable. I let myself down and killed my self-esteem. I let myself be treated like that for seven years.

After the breakup, I completely turned my life around. I became happy just by not having him around. I was nervous to date and didn't think I was ready, but some friends encouraged me to get a Tinder just for fun, and to gain some confidence. Honestly, it did help a lot! I felt desired (minus some weirdos… you know tinder) and confident with myself again. One day I got super liked by this guy, and guess what? That guy is my future husband! I love him so incredibly much. He has taught me what REAL love is and how I should be treated. He is the best thing that has ever happened to me.

Minus the experience of what happened over those seven years; my past relationship taught me so much, and made me the person I am today. It taught me never to settle, never to let someone treat me like shit, to be the bigger person, not to take bullshit, and to go for what I want and not be ashamed of it. I was happy that my past relationship happened, because I honestly believe I wouldn't be where I am today if it wasn't for it.

Come out of heartbreak only with positives, it's the best way.

* * *

"She was the kind of girl- friend God gives you young, so you'll know loss for the rest of your life."
— Junot Diaz

Control Freak

My ex-husband used to be the most amazing boy. I say boy because, after everything, I most definitely cannot call him a man.

Like a lot of couples these days, we met online. He seemed like the perfect guy... almost too good to be true. He was a total babe from the south and he was in the Marines, which at the time was everything I thought I needed in a man. So after talking for a little while, we started dating. One of the main issues was, though, that he lived super far away from me.

When I say super far, I'm talking almost fifteen hours of driving each way. I was the one who mainly did all of the visiting and driving, which was exhausting, but I mean, it's what you do when you're smitten with someone.

Eventually, he proposed to me, and I was over the moon. We still didn't live in the same area, but we were used to it, so it didn't seem like a big obstacle… until it was. He started to get angry with me when I would go and hang out with my friends that he didn't know and couldn't be there to meet. He used to FaceTime me whenever I was hanging out with them, because he didn't believe that I was with who I said I was with. He started to treat me more and more like I was his property, but at the time, I took it as a sweet gesture, reminding myself that he's was only doing those things because he loved me and cared.

We finally got married and spent two fantastic weeks together before he was sent overseas for TWO YEARS. The Marine Corps wouldn't let me move with him even though we were married, so that meant we were about to spend those two years 7,000 miles apart from each other. It was already tough enough to be so far away from him, and even more robust having him control my life even from far away. He wanted to know every single detail about what was going on, which sounds sweet and like he misses me, but in reality, he just wanted full control.

He made me quit my job and wanted me to take online classes so that I wouldn't be out in public, and couldn't talk to people. I was furious at first but then put it in my head that he was just worried about something happening to me when he wasn't there.

February rolled around, and I decided to go and see him. When I was there, he went through my phone, including my Facebook and scolded me after finding messages from my ex-boyfriend, from FIVE years ago. He yelled and told me that it was inappropriate to keep those messages and a slap in the face to him. He told me that I was stupid and irresponsible, which he tended to do every time I did something that he didn't want me to do.

I left to go back home sooner than I had planned, but I was so distraught over how he treated me when I was there that I needed to go before it got worse. All was okay between us for a little while after that, until he disappeared and stopped communicating altogether. I found out that he was drinking and staying at random girls' places, which, as you could have guessed, resulted in him cheating on me multiple times.

When I confronted him about it, he immediately asked for a divorce, saying that I had been cheating on him too, which was the farthest from the truth. I told him that I refused and that we should fight for each other (which was stupid now that I look back at it) but I was still so deep under his power.

The "fighting for each other" lasted a couple of months until I was finally able to snap out of it and realize that I no longer loved him.

I told him that he could have his way with the divorce because he disgusted me and took everything away from me from the very beginning. He threatened to kill himself, though, because gosh forbid, I agree with what he wanted in the first place. The thought of him losing me freaked him out because he wasn't sure how to handle not having someone to control and emotionally abuse.

Once we officially filed for divorce, I immediately felt like an enormous weight was being lifted off of my shoulders. I dropped all connections with him and his family, which was hard at first, but helped me cope quicker (not to say that my coping was a quick thing because it wasn't.) I hid in my room for a long time because I felt lost and didn't know what to do next.

Once I left my room, though, I made new friends, got really into retail therapy, and slowly but surely started to feel like my old self again. Now I am flourishing on the fact that I am an independent woman and can do whatever I want, whenever I want. I learned so much about myself because of that entire experience and can honestly say that for the first time in my life, I love myself for who I am.

If you are in a relationship similar to me, take that step and get out of it. Nobody should be controlling you except for yourself. If they genuinely love you, they would let you strive just the way you are and continuously have you in their best interest. Everyone deserves to love themselves and be loved the correct way. I'm so glad I figured that out and I can't wait for you to figure it out too.

* * *

"And you know what? When the door closes right in your face - when it slams. And you think it's all over. It's not. It's not over. It's the beginning of the rest of your life. So many mad, beautiful moments are right around the corner. Don't give up."

— m. a.

Reliability

I was nineteen and had just come out of a three year, highly depressive and very tumultuous time of my life. I had been held in a very abusive relationship where I was kept in a room for days on end, taken for all my money, dignity, self-respect, and health. I was found unconscious in my dorm room with a dislocated jaw and shoulder, while I was supposed to be at my sister's college graduation. To say I was wary of a relationship after that would be a colossal understatement.

A lot of people neglect to talk about what happens after you get out of an abusive relationship. The most common thing people do is jump into another abusive relationship, whether it be the same or different nature. Personally, I was looking to fill the void that I was left with after ending it with my ex. I ended up finding a man who ended up swiftly stealing my identity and lying to my face.

I recognized what was happening only after I fell further into debt by his actions. I pulled away as fast as I could, and at that point, was desperate to feel like my old self again. Before everything happened, I was excitable, hyper, and hungry for life. I wanted to get back to that as soon as possible.

My sister had met her now-husband on Match.com, so I figured I'd give that a try. It was a bust at first, until it wasn't. The day I went to cancel my account, which was bout six weeks into the membership, I got a message from a sweet ginger man with gorgeous blue eyes, asking to take me to dinner. I was taken aback by his directness, but said yes.

We agreed on going to dinner the week after. He didn't say much between the initial message and the day of our date, but I knew he wanted to pick me up at my parent's house, which is where I was living at the time. He showed up twenty minutes early, and not only was I not dressed, but also had only half of a face of makeup on. I hid in the bathroom to finish getting ready while I sat him in front of a TV, talked to him through a door. The night could not have started on a more awkward note.

We finally left to go to dinner, and the restaurant he picked was so busy we couldn't even turn into the parking lot. At that point, he was lost with what to do, and I started barking orders of where to go. When we finally found a place and got settled, I was very candid and open about my previous relationships, and how I wanted nothing more than to never have to go through that again. He was extremely comforting and seemed to listen.

Later into talking, we figured out that we had met when we were small, due to a mutual family friend. The date took a turn for the better after the super awkward start and I didn't know what would happen afterward, but I knew that my birthday was in three days and I wanted to see him after. That was if he wanted to see me again.

He ended up being the first person to wish me a happy birthday but I absentmindedly ignored his text and only noticed a week later, when I noticed that he hadn't reached out. I sent him a text right away, demanding that he take me out again. That same day, he showed up to my dad's office to pick me up and take me to lunch. He then continued to show up every day before and after work to see me and before I knew it, we saw each other more than we were seeing our friends and family, and it was great.

The next four years were filled with job changes, going back to school, transitioning from local to long-distance, planning our lives together, and also finding our flaws. We rarely fought unless his drinking flared up. When that happened, he would miss significant events and say horrible things to me but I acted like they didn't bother me... until they started to effect prominent elements in my life.

He was supposed to help me move back to my college town where I planned to restart the bachelor's program that I had to drop out of, due to my previous abusive relationship. He was so drunk though, that he couldn't even stand up and I was unable to move in until 10 pm on Sunday night, the night before classes started.

We were in front of his family, another night, and he was beyond trashed. He told me that I was not happy, and truly miserable with every element of my life. He then continued to tell me that I was not capable of loving him or myself, and that he would never be able to stabilize me financially.

While we had those issues to deal with, I also struggled with my anger, stress levels, and getting through my bachelor's program. Not to mention, I had a theatrical family. My sister and boyfriend did not get along, so he refused to go to her wedding or any event that he was invited to with my family, even though I begged him to accompany me.

We tried to talk each hiccup out and both seemed to want it to work. We made the distance work to the best of our ability, but he struggled with my inability to miss class, having to visit more often, and having to do a lot of the traveling to me. We had many talks about our future; having kids and being together forever, but then he told me that our divorce would be inevitable.

I was naive and believed that I could change his mind. He came from a family where divorce was more common than marriage, and he never felt that he could be different than his surroundings. When I graduated from college, I decided that moving to where he was, would not be feasible. The jobs were sparse, and there was nowhere for me to feel "at home." There was no Jewish community within an hour, no family or friends anywhere close, and he was traveling a lot for his job so I would end up being alone a lot.

I chose to move closer to his company's corporate headquarters in Chicago, where he once said he wanted to transfer to. I truly thought that move was best for both of us, but all of a sudden, I was the enemy. I planned my life around this man, thought he would come to me as we had talked about, and only wanted to be with him, yet I was the enemy. His mother had called me six weeks before my move and told me that if our relationship failed, it was 100% my fault and that I should only move somewhere where he was at that very moment.

I kept talking and pleading for him to understand my situation, and that I had a job offer in Chicago. I needed to be close to my family as well. He would go through moments of calm, but his overall sentiment was, "well, you chose to move to the city, and I hate the city, so I will NEVER come to see you."

I told him that I was ready to settle down and wanted to be with him, but he angrily responded, saying that he thought I needed to go to therapy again because no one decides out of the blue that they want to get married.

I was hurt, shattered, and felt my life changing faster than I was ready for it to. The thought that the man I invested five years in didn't think I was worth marrying and thought I was crazy to want to marry him made me sick to my stomach. I was faced with being the bad guy and knowing that I had to be the one to walk away.

He said to me once at the beginning of our relationship that he would never fight for a girl, and he meant it because he did not fight for me to stay. I was not ready to end things, but I knew I needed to. I had to end it with him over FaceTime since he wouldn't come visit.

After the deed was done I remember immediately puking and thinking about how hard it was going to be to start over from there.

I had to challenge myself to do the smallest things each day and relearn how to be myself again. Granted, this was a much different situation from the abuse; I was physically who I was, but emotionally, I was a shell. I would challenge myself to go grocery shopping, walk home without talking to my mom, and try to go on outings alone. It was not easy, and I did ultimately get a therapist to learn coping mechanisms, but I still struggle sometimes and am still learning how to trust that someone is interested in me.

I finally understood, though, that to move forward, you still have to be vulnerable and try things to make your life happen the way YOU want it to.

* * *

"For once in my life, I feel true freedom. Acceptance for everything that is and is not and for everything that is to come."

Forward

Thank you so much for reading these strong girl's stories. I hope that their found strength gave you the courage and knowledge to know that even though heartbreaks suck, you will get through it, and better things will come your way.

Each one of the stories have different backgrounds, but they all had one main thing in common; they came out of their struggles with a better understanding of who they are and gained the confidence to live their lives to the fullest, with or without a partner.

If you still don't feel any better after reading this, let me go ahead and try to boost your self-esteem a little…

• YOU ARE BEAUTIFUL

• YOU ARE WORTH FIGHTING FOR

• YOU DESERVE NOTHING BUT THE BEST

• **YOU ARE SO LOVED**

•**CHOCOLATE IS CALORIE FREE WHEN YOU'RE SAD**

• **THE BEST REVENGE IS TO LIVE WELL AND SMILE DOING IT**

I love all of you!